Oh Dear Me, I'm Late for Tea!

Written by Alison Hawes

Illustrated by Mike Phillips

Collins

4

6

9

12

13

14

Ideas for guided reading

Learning objectives: Understanding and using terms about books and print; using knowledge of familiar texts to re-enact or retell to others; knowing that books are ordered left to right; learning new words from their reading and shared experiences; listening to and making environmental sounds

Curriculum links: Creative development: Using their imagination in role play and stories; Knowledge and understanding of the world: Finding out about objects they observe

Getting started

- Introduce the book, using the terms cover, title, author and illustrator. Show how you read the title, pointing to each word. Ask the children to 'have a go'.

- Looking at the cover, say that you can see Granny is in a hurry. Can the children say how you know? Do the children know about watches? Ask children to say what might happen in the story.

- Turn to the title page and ask the children why Granny is in a hurry. If necessary, tell them that someone's birthday party tea is at 3 o'clock. Discuss why it is important to be on time for a birthday party and ask the children whose party they think it is.

Reading and responding

- Ask the children to go through the pages in order from p2 to p13, and describe what is happening. As the children talk about the story, introduce words that extend their vocabulary, e.g. *parachute, skateboard, helmet*.

- Ask children to investigate the illustrations and prompt children to comment on the clock faces. Check that they follow the story from left to right before looking in more detail.